RUBY'S NEW HOME

by **Tony** and **Lauren Dungy**

illustrated by

Vanessa Brantley Newton

Ready-to-Read

Simon Spotlight

New York London Toronto Sydney New Delhi

To our children: Tiara, James, Eric, Jordan, Jade, Justin, and Jason —T. D. and L. D.

"And do not forget to do good and to share with others, for with such sacrifices God is pleased."
—Hebrews 13:16 (NIV)

SIMON SPOTLIGHT
An imprint of Simon & Schuster Children's Publishing Division
1230 Avenue of the Americas, New York, New York 10020
Text copyright © 2011 by Tony Dungy and Lauren Dungy
Illustrations copyright © 2011 by Vanessa Brantley Newton
Published in association with the literary agency of Legacy, LLC, Winter Park, FL 32789
All rights reserved, including the right of reproduction in whole or in part in any form.
SIMON SPOTLIGHT, READY-TO-READ, and colophon are registered trademarks of Simon & Schuster, Inc.
For information about special discounts for bulk purchases, please contact Simon & Schuster Special Sales at 1-866-506-1949 or business@simonandschuster.com.
Manufactured in the United States of America 0711 LAK
First Edition 10 9 8 7 6 5 4 3 2 1
Library of Congress Cataloging-in-Publication Data
Dungy, Tony.
Ruby's new home / by Tony and Lauren Dungy. — 1st ed.
p. cm. — (Ready-to-read)
Summary: When Jordan, Justin, and Jade get a new dog, they must learn to share the work of caring for her, as well as her love.
[1. Dog adoption—Fiction. 2. Dogs—Fiction. 3. Sharing—Fiction. 4. Family life—Fiction.] I. Dungy, Lauren. II. Title.
PZ7.D9186Rub 2011
[E]—dc22
2010054463
ISBN 978-1-4169-9784-9 (pbk)
ISBN 978-1-4424-2948-2 (hc)
ISBN 978-1-4424-3515-5 (eBook)

Everyone was excited!
Mom and Dad had a big surprise.
Today was the day Ruby would
arrive. The kids could not wait to
meet their new dog.

After lunch Mom and Dad brought Ruby home. "Everyone has to learn to share," Mom said. "We will all have to take care of Ruby."

"Isn't she cute?" Jade said.
"Ruby is going to be so much fun,"
said Jordan.
Justin smiled and nodded.
Everyone loved Ruby right away!

Mom took them to the pet store.
She told each of them they could
pick out something special for
Ruby.

Jade picked out a leash
and bowl.

Jordan picked out a ball and blanket.
Justin picked out a collar and a tag.
Then he picked out a box of treats
for Ruby. Everything was red!
"Why did you all pick red?"
asked Mom.

"Her name is Ruby," said Jade.
"So red is her favorite color!"
Mom smiled. "I am glad we are
all sharing Ruby
so well," she said.

That night Mom heard loud voices. She walked down the hall to see what was going on. Justin was hugging Ruby.

Jordan was holding her ball.
And Jade was trying to pull Ruby
with her leash!

"What is going on here?" asked
Mom.

Jordan said, "Ruby is *my* dog.
I want her to sleep in my room."

Justin said, "No, Ruby is my dog. I want her to sleep in my room."

Jade said, "Mom, they are both wrong. Ruby is my dog, and she should sleep in my room."

Just then Ruby barked.
They all let go of Ruby and looked
at Mom.

"Ruby is a member of our family,"
Mom said. "We need to share her.
There is plenty of fun to go around.
Ruby loves all of you. Right, Ruby?"

Everyone looked around. "Where is Ruby now?" asked Justin. Where did Ruby go? She was nowhere in sight!

They looked in Jordan's room.
No Ruby.

They looked in Jade's room.
No Ruby.

They looked in Justin's room.
No Ruby!

Then they looked downstairs.

Ruby was curled up in her crate
on her brand-new red blanket!
She was fast asleep.
"It looks like Ruby has found
her own spot to sleep," said Mom.

The next morning Dad
had a good idea.
"Let's have a picnic
at the park," he said.

"Can Ruby come too?" asked Jade.
"We can all play with her together!"
"I will bring Ruby's leash,"
said Justin.

"I will bring her ball," said Jordan.

"And I will bring her treats," said
Jade.

They all took turns playing with Ruby. They all threw the ball for her to chase.

They took turns holding the leash
to keep her safely near them.
They all gave her treats
but not too many!

On the drive home Ruby fell
asleep in the back seat.
She was so tired she was snoring!

"Look, Mom," said Justin.
"Sweet little Ruby really is our
dog!"
Mom smiled. "Isn't sharing fun? We
can share taking care of Ruby, and
share playing with Ruby."

"Best of all," said Dad,
"we can share Ruby's love, too!"